Borealis is an imprint
of White Wolf Publishing.

White Wolf Publishing
735 Park North Boulevard, Suite 128
Clarkston, GA 30021
USA
World Wide Web Page: www.white-wolf.com

Book design by Dave McKean @ Hourglass

Wanted: One halibut, must be in good working order, own fins, no skate please.

Will swap two infants, one called Yolanda, one called Liam, both house trained, except Liam.

Offers to Mr. David Tench McKean Esq. c/o The Publisher.

The DAY i swapped my DAD for TWO goldfisH

neil Gaiman & dave McKean

Lost: One book. If found please return to Hayley Campbell (although she may be too big for it)

or Maddy Gaiman (although it may be too big for her).

No fish, please.

One day my mom went out and left me at home with just my little sister and my dad.

My dad sat in front of the television, reading his newspaper. My dad doesn't pay much attention to anything, when he's reading his newspaper.

My little sister and I played in the garden.
My sister played with her Barbie dolls,
and I played at putting mud down my sister's neck.

My friend Nathan came
over to my house.

He had a glass bowl with him.
There was something in the glass bowl.

"What's that?"
(I said.)

"Two Goldfish,"
(he said). "They are
called Sawney and Beaney.
Aren't they neat?"

We went up to my bedroom.
My little sister tagged along.
I showed Nathan my old transformer
robots, and my baseball cards, and my books.
I showed him my old punching bag and my
penny whistle that Mommy said made her
head ache when I blew it. I showed him
my old spaceship that didn't float in the
bath any more, and the puppet with the
tangled strings, and I even showed him
Clownie, my clown that I sleep with.

I thought for a bit.

Some people have great ideas maybe once or twice in their life, and then they discover electricity or fire or outer space or something.
I mean, the Kind of brilliant ideas that change the whole world.

Some people never have them at all.

When my mother came home I said, "Mom, can we buy some goldfish food?"

My mother looked at me sharply.

"Right", said my mother, and she picked up the bowl of goldfish and handed it to me. "You can take these goldfish over to Nathan this minute, and don't you come back without your father."

"I told you so," said my little sister.

"And you can go with him," said my mother. "Fancy allowing your brother to swap your father for two goldfish and a bowl. The very idea."

So we went to Nathan's house.
He only lives over the road.
I knocked on the door.

Nathan's mother came out.

Is Nathan here? I asked.

"Where did you get those goldfish," she asked me.

"They were a present to Nathan from his Aunt Violet."

"I swapped them," I said. "And now I have to swap them back again."

Blinky had a very big house.
We went up to the front and rang the bell.

The butler came out.

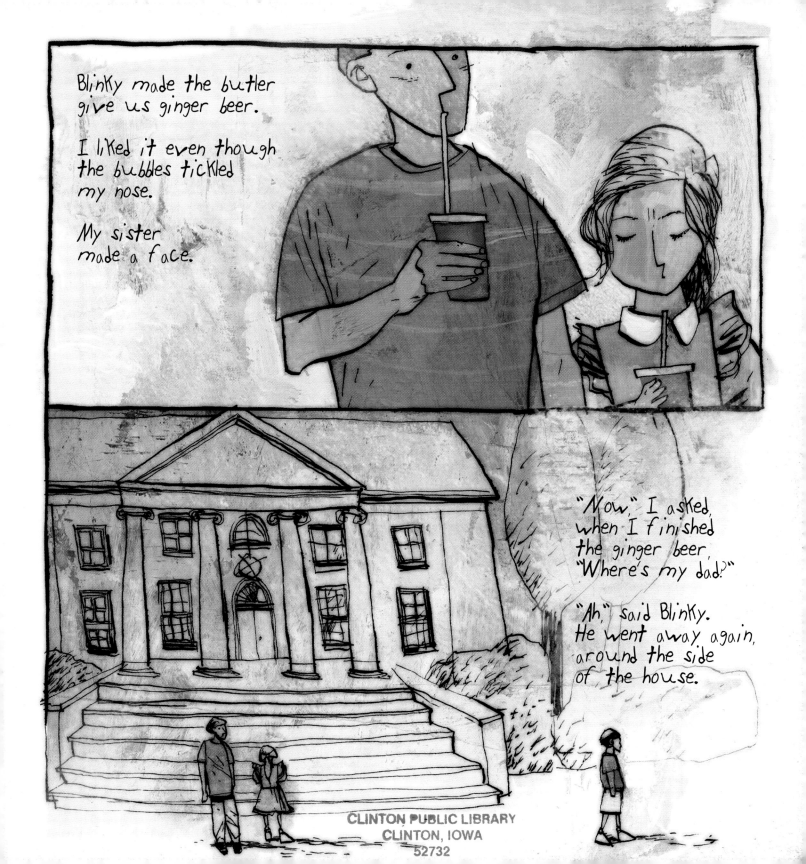

Blinky made the butler give us ginger beer.

I liked it even though the bubbles tickled my nose.

My sister made a face.

"Now," I asked, when I finished the ginger beer, "Where's my dad?"

"Ah," said Blinky. He went away again, around the side of the house.

I gave him the gorilla mask. He gave me Galveston and a map he drew of how to get to Patti's house.

I'd never walked so far in my whole life.

While we walked, Galveston the Rabbit sat in my arms and made its nose go woffly. My sister tried to make her nose go as woffly as Galveston's but she couldn't do it.

There was a little rabbit hutch there,
and next to the rabbit hutch was a little
run with chicken wire all around it.
My dad sat on the grass, in the chicken wire run,
reading his newspaper and eating a carrot.
He looked a bit lonely, and he had grass all
over his trousers.

Last week my little sister told everyone at school that I was adopted. The week before she told everyone at school that I was a space alien pretending to be me.

When we got home my mother said things like, "Just look at the state of him!" and she made him go and have a bath and she put all his clothes into the washing.

While dad was in the bath, my mother told me off.

And when she'd finished
telling me off, she made
me promise cross-my-
heart, that I would
never - ever - swap
my dad for anything
ever ever again.

And I promised.

So I won't.

But I never promised anything
about my little sister...